For Rikka

First American Edition 2016
Kane Miller, A Division of EDC Publishing

Text and illustrations © 2015 Jez Alborough

Published by arrangement with Walker Books Ltd
87 Vauxhall Walk, London SE11 5HJ

For information contact:
Kane Miller, A Division of EDC Publishing
PO Box 470663
Tulsa, OK 74147-0663
www.kanemiller.com
www.edcpub.com
www.usbornebooksandmore.com

Library of Congress Control Number: 2015954193

Printed in Malaysia
2 3 4 5 6 7 8 9 10
ISBN: 978-1-61067-476-8

Albert
and Little Henry

JEZ ALBOROUGH

Kane Miller
A DIVISION OF EDC PUBLISHING

When Albert was little, he loved having stories read to him.

When he grew bigger, he started making up stories of his own.

Albert's mom and dad loved to hear his stories,
but one day everything changed...

That was the day that Little Henry arrived.

"I can't listen to a story now," said Dad.
"Little Henry needs his bath."

"Not now, Albie," said Mom.
"I'm trying to get Little Henry off to sleep."

"We're a bit tired now, Albie," whispered Mom.
"Why don't you tell us a story later?"

So Albert went to his room to wait for later to come.
Then something very strange happened...

He started
to feel
small.

The next day, which was the day of Little Henry's party,

Albert felt even smaller. But the odd thing was,

no one seemed to notice how small he'd become.

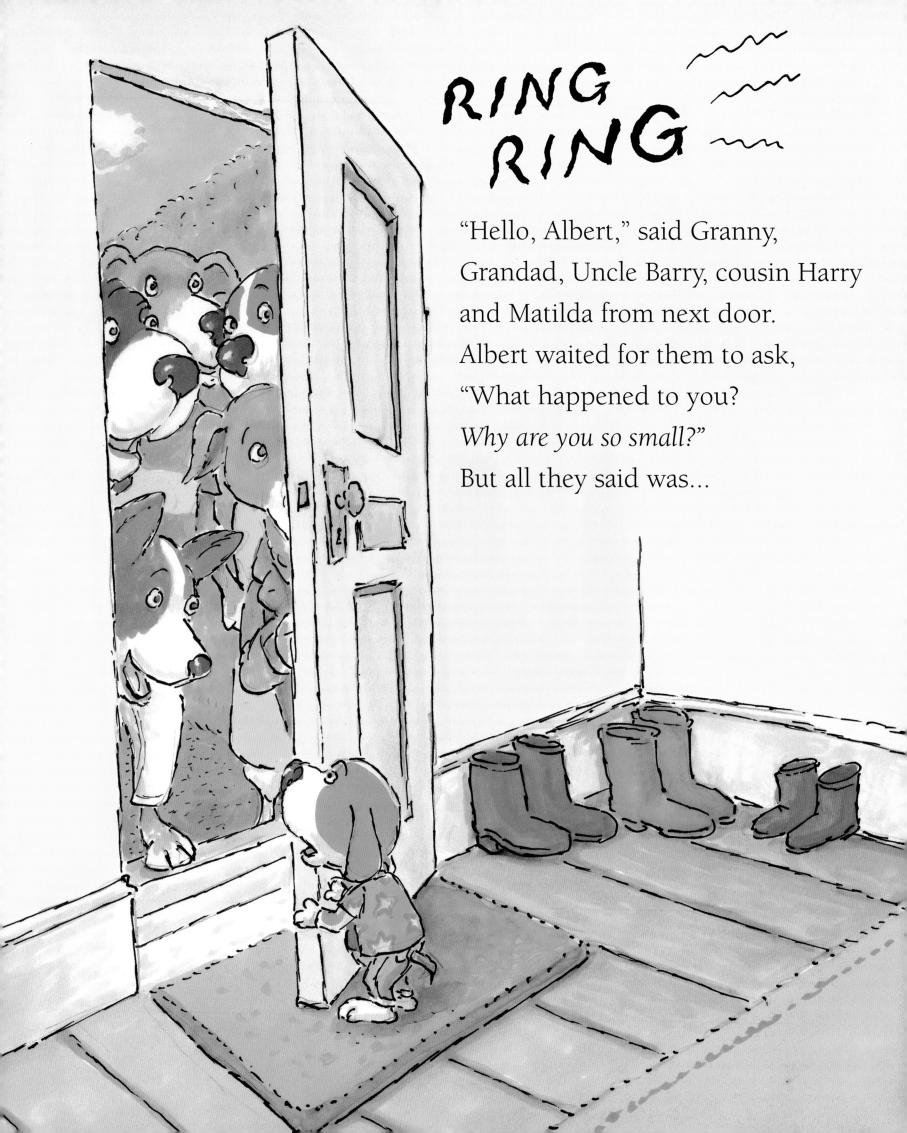

RING
RING

"Hello, Albert," said Granny,
Grandad, Uncle Barry, cousin Harry
and Matilda from next door.
Albert waited for them to ask,
"What happened to you?
Why are you so small?"
But all they said was...

"LITTLE HENRY!" said Albert as his tail started to twitch.

"LITTLE HENRY!" said Albert as he stomped off to his bedroom.

"Are you in there, sweetheart?" said Albert's mom.

"We were all wondering where you had gone."

"I've got a present for you.
I'll leave it by the door.
Come out when you're ready."

The present was a book,
a very special book.
The pages were all blank,

but on the cover he found
three magical words:

for Albert's stories.

That was when Albert
stopped feeling small.

Albert ran back to the living room.

Thank you for my present.

"Look, Albie," said Dad. "Little Henry wants you to hold him."

So Albert did.

"Albert," said Dad, "will you tell me a story?"
"I'd like to hear one too," said Granny. Then Grandad,
Uncle Barry, cousin Harry and Matilda from next door
all agreed. So Albert had a think.

And, from that day on, Albert never felt small again.